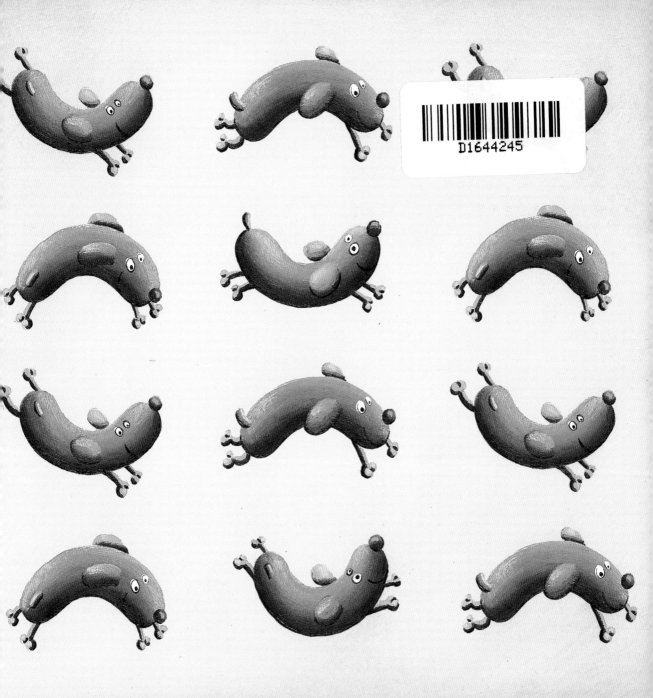

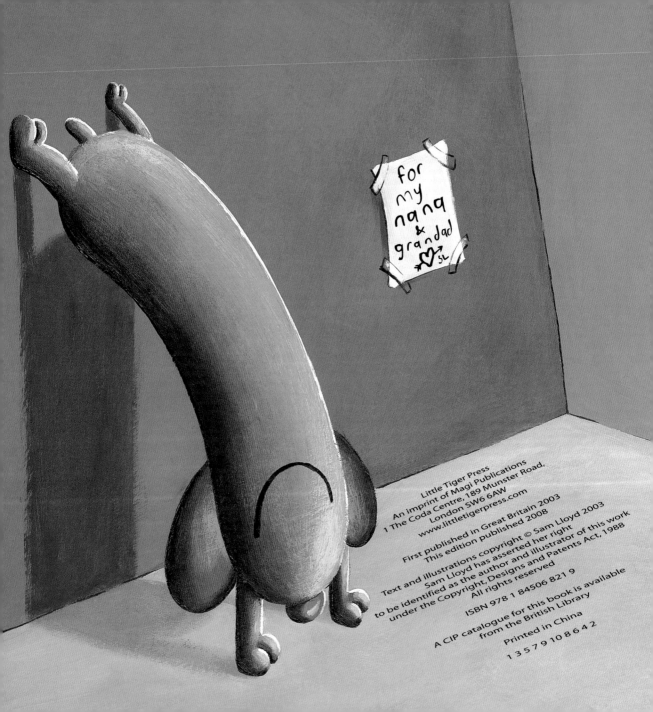

Little Tiger Press
An imprint of Magi Publications
1 The Coda Centre, 189 Munster Road,
London SW6 6AW
www.littletigerpress.com

First published in Great Britain 2003
This edition published 2008

Text and illustrations copyright © Sam Lloyd 2003
Sam Lloyd has asserted her right
to be identified as the author and illustrator of this work
under the Copyright, Designs and Patents Act, 1988

ISBN 978 1 84506 821 9

A CIP catalogue for this book is available
from the British Library

Printed in China

1 3 5 7 9 10 8 6 4 2

SUPER SID
THE SILLY SAUSAGE DOG

Sam Lloyd

LITTLE TIGER PRESS
LONDON

Sid was a sausage dog who lived
in the kennels on the edge of town.
He lived there because he didn't have
a nice kind owner to love and care
for him like other dogs.

Sid wanted a nice
kind owner more than
anything. So he decided
to find one for himself!

First Sid took a giant leap
over the kennel wall, to show
what a good jumper he was . . .

But . . .

. . . he landed on top
of Madam Murples'
very posh tea party.

"Silly Sid!"
screeched the ladies.
"Back to the kennels
at once!"

Then Sid tried to show
everyone what a good
digger he was.

But . . .

. . . he dug up all Gardener
Pete's prize vegetables.

"Silly Sid!" growled Pete. "Now I'll never win the best vegetable competition. Back to the kennels with you!"

"I know," thought Sid. "I'll show
everyone what a good singer I am.
That will cheer them up."
He howled and howled as loud as
his doggy lungs would let him.

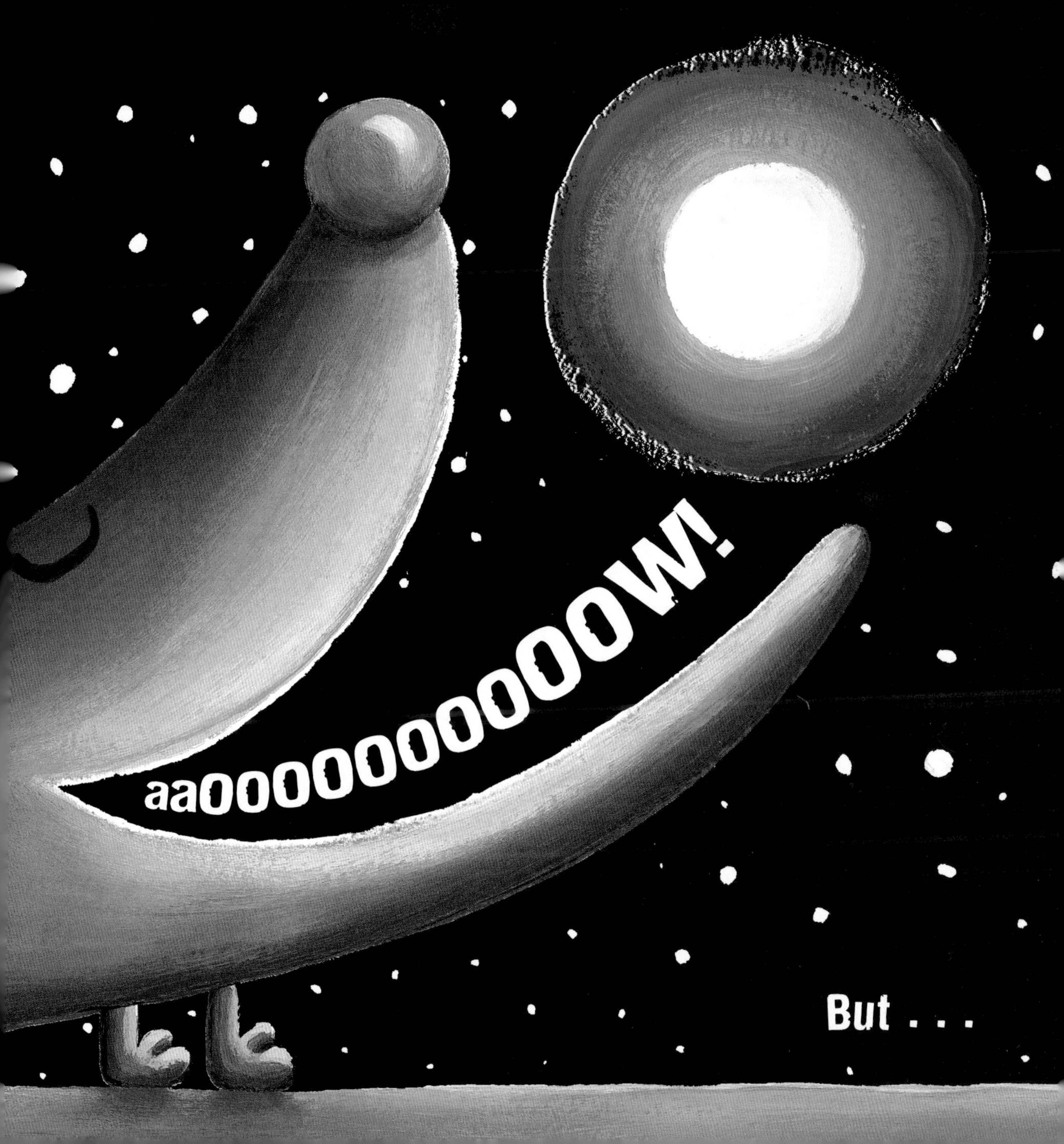

But . . .

. . . he woke the whole street!
"SILLY SID!"
they cried, throwing water at him.
"Go away!"

Poor Sid. Sad, wet and lonely
he crept back to the kennels.
"Nobody wants me," he thought.
"I'll never find a proper home."

The next morning Sid was woken by a very

strange smell. He put his nose into the air and, without thinking, he followed the smell . . .

through the garden, around the bird table until at last he came to...

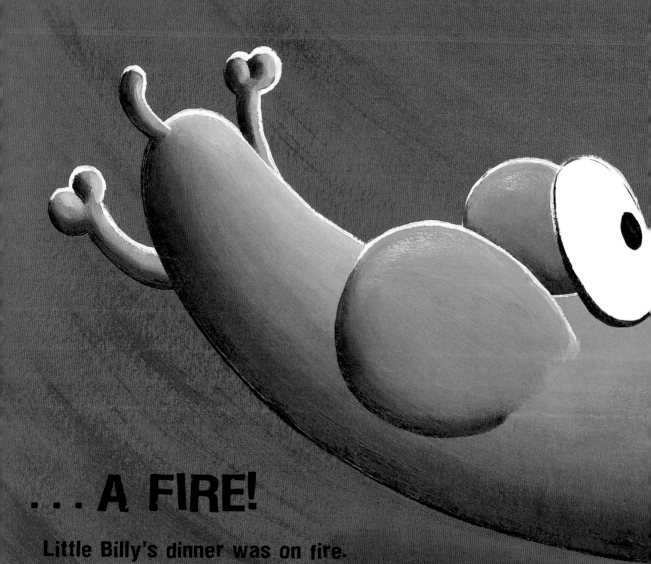

. . . A FIRE!

Little Billy's dinner was on fire.
Grandma had forgotten all about it.

aaOOOOOOOOW!

Sid jumped up and down
and he sang and he woofed.
And he howled as loud as
his doggy lungs would
let him. Until . . .

. . . the fireman came and, with a rush and a gush and a great big splash, he put the fire out!

"Clever Sid," said Grandma.
"Brave Sid," said the fireman.
"Super Sid," said the crowd.

"My Sid!" said Little Billy.

So Sid had found not
one but two of the nicest,
kindest owners **ever!**

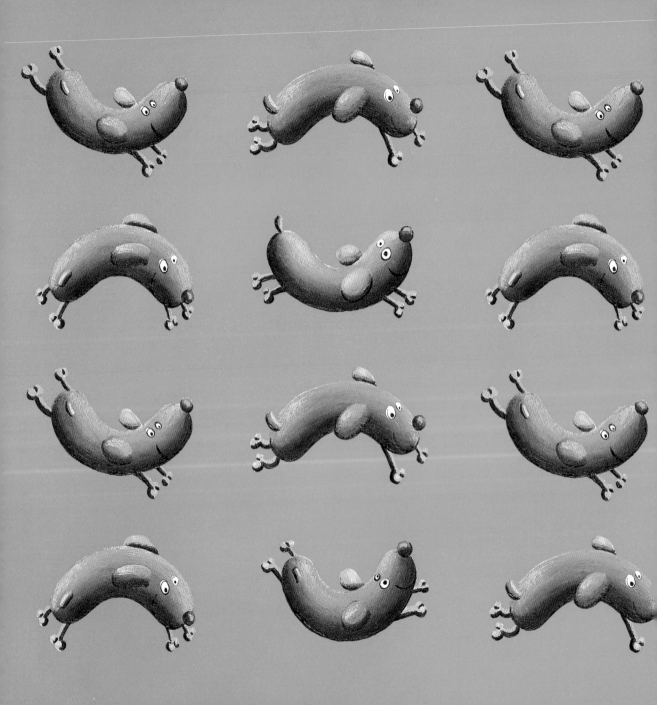